PEDRO

PIRATE
PEDRO

by Fran Manushkin

illustrated by
Tammie Lyon

PICTURE WINDOW BOOKS
a capstone imprint

Pedro is published by Picture Window Books,
a Capstone Imprint
1710 Roe Crest Drive
North Mankato, Minnesota 56003
www.mycapstone.com

Text © 2017 Fran Manushkin
Illustrations © 2017 Picture Window Books

Library of Congress Cataloging-in-Publication Data
Names: Manushkin, Fran, author. | Lyon, Tammie, illustrator.
Title: Pirate Pedro / by Fran Manushkin; illustrated by Tammie Lyon.
Description: North Mankato, Minnesota: Picture Window Books, a Capstone
    imprint, [2017] | Series: Pedro | Summary: On Pirate Day at school, all
    the children dress up as pirates, and Pedro and his friends, Katie and
    JoJo, continue the theme in their clubhouse after school—but they all
    want to be the pirate captain.
Identifiers: LCCN 2016033111| ISBN 9781515808725 (library binding) | ISBN
    9781515808749 (pbk.) | ISBN 9781515808800 (ebook (pdf))
Subjects: LCSH: Hispanic American boys—Juvenile fiction. | Pirates—Juvenile
    fiction. | Friendship—Juvenile fiction. | Play—Juvenile fiction. | CYAC:
    Hispanic Americans—Fiction. | Pirates—Fiction. | Friendship—Fiction. |
    Play—Fiction.
Classification: LCC PZ7.M3195 Pk 2017 | DDC 813.54 [E] —dc23
LC record available at https://lccn.loc.gov/2016033111

Designers: Tracy McCabe
Design Elements: Shutterstock

Printed and bound in the USA.
112017   010943R

Table of Contents

Chapter 1
Pirate Day

"Ahoy there! Wake up!"

said Pedro's dad. "It's Pirate

Day at school."

Pedro got up fast.

He ate his pirate pancakes

and put on his pirate hat.

"Good-bye," Pedro said.

"See you later, landlubbers!"

"Take me along!" said Paco.

"You are too little," said Pedro.

Peppy, Pedro's puppy, tried to come too.

"No way!" said Pedro.

"Puppies can't be pirates."

At school, Miss Winkle
said, "Hello, crew! Are you
ready to be pirates?"

"Arrr!" yelled Pedro and
Katie and JoJo.

"Can you unscramble these pirate words?" asked Miss Winkle.

"*Glaf* is flag!" said Pedro. "And *words* is sword!"

"Right-o!" said Miss Winkle.

During art, Pedro made a

pirate flag.

"It's called a Jolly

Roger," said Katie. "They

named it after a happy

man named Roger."

JoJo told the class a story about a girl pirate.

"Her name was Mary Read," said JoJo. "She was fierce!"

After school, Pedro said, "Let's be pirates at my house."

"Arrr!" yelled Katie. "I'll be the captain. I'm fierce — just like Mary Read!"

"No way!" said Pedro. "Being captain is my job."

Chapter 2
Pirates at Pedro's

Pedro's clubhouse was their

ship. He proudly put up the

Jolly Roger.

"I want to be a pirate too!"

yelled Paco. He put on an eye

patch and began running

around.

"Watch out!" warned JoJo.

"You are walking the plank!"

JoJo grabbed Paco before

he fell overboard!

"I think fast," JoJo bragged.

"That's why I should be the

captain."

"No! I should be captain,"
said Katie. "I have sharper
eyes. I can see a crow sitting
on our crow's nest."

"But I am strong," said

Pedro. "And brave! See my

sword? I can win any fight!"

Chapter 3
Who Will Be Captain?

Suddenly, it began to rain.

"Don't worry," said Pedro.

"My ship is strong! It will keep

us dry through any storm."

Below the ship, Peppy was
rolling in the mud.

Oops! Pedro dropped his
sword — into the puddle.

Peppy picked it up to fetch

it. He was a good fetcher.

"No!" yelled Pedro. "It is

not a stick. Don't bring it back

to me."

Did Peppy listen? No! He climbed the ladder and shook mud all over the pirates!

"Shiver me timbers!" shouted

Pedro. "It's fun getting wet!"

"For sure!" yelled Katie,

laughing.

"Yes!" said JoJo. "We are jolly

pirates."

"We would
all be jolly
captains," said
Pedro. "Maybe
we should take
turns."

"I thought
of that too,"
said Katie.

"So did I!"
said JoJo.

Soon it was time for a snack of hot dogs and pirate grog.

All the pirates agreed: it was very tasty!

About the Author

Fran Manushkin is the author
of many popular picture books,
including *Happy in Our Skin*; *Baby,
Come Out!*; *Latkes and Applesauce:
A Hanukkah Story*; *The Tushy
Book*; *Big Girl Panties*; and *Big
Boy Underpants*. Fran writes on
her beloved Mac computer in New York City,
without the help of her two naughty cats,
Chaim and Goldy.

About the Illustrator

Tammie Lyon began her love for
drawing at a young age while
sitting at the kitchen table with
her dad. She continued her love
of art and eventually attended
the Columbus College of Art
and Design, where she earned
a bachelor's degree in fine art. After a brief
career as a professional ballet dancer, she decided
to devote herself full-time to illustration. Today she
lives with her husband, Lee, in Cincinnati, Ohio.
Her dogs, Gus and Dudley, keep her company as she
works in her studio.

Glossary

crow's nest (KROHZ NEST)—a small platform used for a lookout, found on top of the mast of a sailing ship

fierce (FEERS)—daring and dangerous

grog (GROG)—a juice that pirates like to drink

landlubbers (LAND-luh-bers)—people who live on the land and know little or nothing about the sea

overboard (OH-vur-bord)—over the side of a boat and into the water

walking the plank (WAWK-ing THUH PLANGK)—forced to walk along a board sticking out over the side of the ship and fall into the sea

Let's Talk

1. Pedro and his friends celebrate Pirate Day at school. What activities did they have? If you could celebrate something at school, what would it be? What kind of activities would you do?

2. Pedro talks like a pirate several times in the story. What are some of the words he uses? Try talking like a pirate yourself.

3. Pedro thinks that a good captain is strong and brave. What else makes a good captain?

Let's Write

1. Pedro is prepared for Pirate Day at school. Write about how you would prepare for Pirate Day. What would you wear?

2. Pedro and his friends decide to take turns being captain. Write about a time you and your friends took turns.

3. Pedro and his friends are jolly pirates and decide to be jolly captains. Look up the word *jolly* and write out the definition. Then write out any other words that mean the same thing.

JOKE AROUND

☠ Why couldn't the pirate go to the movie?
It was rated arrrr.

☠ Why did the pirate buy the eye patch?
He didn't have enough money for an iPad.

☠ Why did it take the pirate so long to learn his alphabet?
He spent years at C.

☠ When is the best time for a pirate to buy their ship?
When it's on sail.

☠ Why can't pirates play cards?
They are sitting on the deck.

WITH PEDRO!

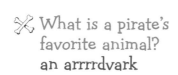

✂ What is a pirate's
favorite animal?
an arrrrdvark

✂ Why are pirates such good singers?
Because they can hit the high Cs!

✂ How much does it cost a pirate to
pierce his ear?
a buccaneer

✂ What are pirates
afraid of?
the darrrrk

✂ What is a pirate's
least favorite
vegetable?
a leek

THE FUN DOESN'T STOP HERE!

Discover more at www.capstonekids.com

✂ Videos & Contests
✂ Games & Puzzles
✂ Friends & Favorites
✂ Authors & Illustrators

Find cool websites and more books like
this one at www.facthound.com. Just type
in the Book ID: 9781515808725 and
you're ready to go!